To James, with love – E.D

THE FROG PRINCESS

by Jan Ormerod and Emma Damon

British Library Cataloguing in Publication Data

A catalogue record of this book is available from the British Library.

ISBN 0 340 87371 x (HB)
ISBN 0 340 87372 8 (PB)

First edition published 2004

10 9 8 7 6 5 4 3 2

Published by Hodder Children's Books
a division of Hodder Headline Limited
338 Euston Road London NW1 3BH

Printed in China

The Frog Princess

Written by
Jan Ormerod

Illustrated by
Emma Damon

h

Hodder
Children's
Books

A division of Hodder Headline Limited

Once upon a time, there was a princess
and a frog who became best friends.

It happened like this.

Princess was always playing near the pond,
and one day PLOP! in fell her golden ball.
As she peered into the pond to find the ball she
saw a pair of big green eyes looking back at her.

She liked
what she saw.

Froggie said, 'Nice ball, Princess.'
She replied, 'You can keep my ball, Froggie,
but only if you promise to let me play
with you and eat at your place and
sleep at your house three times.'

'OK,' said Froggie. He swam away
with the golden ball.
Then Princess called,

**'Stop, Froggie,
remember what you promised.'**

And she leapt into the pond
and dog-paddled about,
until the water cleared and
she saw Froggie hanging around
with his family near the water lilies.

She said, 'Let me stay,
my small slimy one.

Remember to keep
your promise.'

Froggie's father insisted that he be polite to his visitor. So though she was very big and horribly pale and had a little pink mouth like a rose bud, Froggie tried not to show his distaste.

But when she
wanted to share
his food he found
it very hard.

She said, 'Let me eat
with you, my tiddly one.

Remember to keep your promise.'

The sight of delicious delicacies disappearing into that pink mouth made him feel ill.  **YUK!**

But his father gave him a stern look and he remembered his manners.

She said, 'Let me stay over, my wee wet one.
Remember to keep your promise.'
The sight of Princess floating in the duckweed
in her ridiculous big skirts made him want
to giggle, but he kept his promise.

As dawn came, she heaved herself
out of the pond and left, dragging
her sodden skirts behind her.

That afternoon, Princess
came again. She was more
suitably dressed this time
and Froggie couldn't help
admiring her butterfly stroke.

She hung around...

...shared his meal
and slept over...

...then squelched off
in the morning.

The third time Princess came, Froggie was pleased to see her. They played on the grass with the golden ball and had a diving competition. They were so ravenous by teatime that Froggie didn't mind seeing her eat.

Then they told each other jokes
as they floated in the moonlight,
waiting for sleep.

When Froggie awoke,
he found himself sad and
lonely because Princess
had already gone.

And he cried,
'Where is my friend, my big pink girl?

I didn't break my promise!'

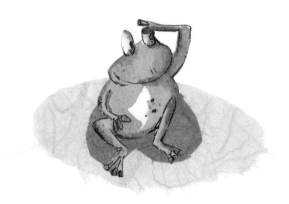

And a voice said, 'Here I am, my little green friend. Here I am... I'm a Frogess.'

And Froggie saw that Princess had become a dinky Frogess.

And he liked what he saw.

Frogess explained that she had been
enchanted by a wicked wizard.
And how Froggie had broken the spell.

He had been friendly
to her as a princess.

And let her eat at his place.

And allowed her to sleep
over three times.

Naturally, Froggie and Frogess were best of friends and lived together in that deep dark pond happily ever after.